THE LOST OASIS OF LOVE

ARLA JONES

ARLA JONES

the Lost Oasis of LOVE

Book Cover by Elani Roman

Editor: Kate Seger

Header by TMT Cover Design

2nd edition 2024

Acknowledgements

I would like to thank my editor Kate Seger, TMT Cover Design for the lovely header image, and Elani Roman for the cover art.

Contents

1

THE SANDSTORM

L illian was a young archeologist invited to join the group of archeologists in Egypt. They had found a new tomb and started excavation there.

Lillian was a beautiful young female with long dark hair and an oval face Jack was his brother who wanted to join her on this trip. However, it was the 1940s and the time of WWII, and also Germans were interested in archeological discoveries. They wanted the treasures for the leaders of the Nazi party. Roy Sawyer was a handsome smuggler who joined Lillian and Jack providing them with transportation. Unwillingly, the archeologists had released a demon called Dina, who wanted to rule the earth, however, Lillian, Jack, and Sawyer managed to send her back to the underworld.

While Sawyer and Lillian escaped from the venomous dunes and the German soldiers, the sandstorm hit, separating them from Lillian's brother Jack. The storm had hit so fast that they immediately lost sight of Jack. The wind swirled around them, and they couldn't see where to go.

Sawyer pulled down his desert scarf to cover his face and hoped the storm would not last long. He had thought they went in the same direction, but he didn't see Jack anywhere. They got off the camels and looked around. Nothing to see. The storm was blowing the sand all over, and everything looked the same.

"Lay down next to the camels," Sawyer ordered Lillian, who did as she was told.

The only way to survive this storm was to cover their bodies as much as possible, so Sawyer grabbed a blanket, threw it over them, and then lay close to Lillian. Sawyer grabbed Lillian, pressed her under him, and covered her face so the stinging sand would not hurt her more. They had their two camels against the wind side, but that didn't block much of the sand. Under him, Lillian had her cotton scarf around her head.

"Will we survive?" Lillian cried, her voice almost disappearing into the howling wind.

"Yes, we will," Sawyer replied, shouting into her ear because otherwise, she would not have heard his answer.

The powerful, turbulent wind howled and swirled the sand around them. Sawyer worried that Jack, alone in the desert, would be disoriented and get lost. Jack was a Londoner, and although he had traveled with his sister to different archeological locations, he was not used to the desert like he was. Sawyer had encountered many sandstorms while serving in the Foreign League.

Sawyer couldn't estimate how long the sandstorm lasted, but eventually, the storm winded down. He pushed the sand-covered blanket away from their bodies, which was heavy with all the sand piled on top. The camels had disappeared sometime during the storm, not that he missed them that much. They were not as fast and reliable as a

Jeep, but now they didn't have either. The camels had been a good choice to travel to the dunes, but in the storm, they had panicked and decided to leave them alone.

Perhaps, they knew a safer place to go, Sawyer thought.

"What is it?" Lillian asked with a crackling voice, then coughed the sand from her mouth and wiped her face.

"The camels have run away. We don't have any transportation, and the scenery has changed." Sawyer gestured around them. The dunescape was different from before. The sandstorm had reformed the dunes, and it looked nothing like where they had been before. He wasn't even sure which way they came or where Dina's tomb was.

Sawyer glanced up his hands on his hips. The sky was dark. The sun was setting, but he couldn't see the stars yet. He wasn't sure if he remembered how to find his north based on the stars.

"Do you know where we are?" Lillian asked and stood up. She brushed the sand from her clothes.

"No, I'm not sure," Sawyer replied.

"And all the water is gone with the camels! We have nothing to drink, and we are in the middle of the desert!"

Lillian said, horrified. She didn't want to die of dehydration after all they had been through with Dina, her tomb, and the dunes. No, that would be a tragedy. She wanted to enjoy life, not die in this endless desert.

"We have to travel by night. It's cooler. I need to refresh my memory and try to remember how to find my way with the stars in the sky," Sawyer said. He had done it before in an area where the landmarks were not visible.

He grabbed Lillian by the hand and said, "I need to find the brightest star in the sky. That's our guiding star. We'll call it the north star." Lillian nodded.

Sawyer continued explaining, "When we proceed in a north-easterly direction during our night trekking, we keep this star in front of us, and we keep sight of the star with it on the right of our head. When dawn comes, we mark the direction we are heading on the ground. I said north, but we could go any direction from here. I don't know where we are now."

He glanced at the sky. The stars were not visible yet. He knew that the Milky Way would show brightly when the night came. Then they could position themselves accordingly, but would that be enough? He was not sure. He knew this was how the Beduins traveled without land-marks.

"I don't know either," Lillian replied. "Let's go that way." She pointed with her hand ahead of her, and they started walking. Dusk was settling. The sun was sinking behind the horizon.

2

AFTER THE STORM

T he strong winds had calmed down, and the night was cool with a starry sky. The stars looked brighter than anywhere else Lillian had seen.

"My eyes are still itchy, and my throat is burning," Lillian complained to Sawyer as they trotted along the endless dunes. Each step was forgiving as the soft sand fell away under their feet and created an impression of their shoes. *One step forward, half step back because the sand pulls you backward*, Lillian thought.

It was a frightening trek. She wished they had water. She knew she couldn't last long with a dry throat and burning eyes. She could easily see the direction where the wind had blown because the dunes had a windward side and then a slip-face side but would it help them to figure out where to go? *No*, she thought. *Because they had lost track of where they had come from.* Wherever she looked, she only saw dune after dune. *A monotonous view, if anything*, she thought.

Soft sand hiking was tiresome. Sawyer glanced at Lillian and noticed how her steps were getting shorter, and she was swaying as if she was going to pass out or fall soon. *She needs water*, Sawyer thought. She wouldn't survive long if we didn't find water, and he had no idea where they could find a river or an oasis. He had no maps because most of the maps were in the vehicle that Jack took, and their camels had some maps in the saddlebags, but the camels were gone too. *What a bad luck day we've had.* Sawyer cursed to himself. *If only Jack would come back looking for us now that the storm is over... But we don't know if he survived the storm. He might have because the Jeep was faster than a camel, but there is no guarantee.*

A cool breeze started, and Lillian shivered. The sun was no longer reflecting from the sand; thus, it felt chilly at night. She tried to lick her lips, but they were dry and cracked. Besides, she didn't have any saliva to lick. She felt exhausted to the point of passing out and lying down on the sand. The only thing that kept her walking forward was that Sawyer kept a keen eye on her, and she didn't want to look like she was a weak woman. She knew she couldn't pretend for much longer. Her legs felt heavy, and her steps were more unsure. More than once, she almost fell, and Sawyer grabbed her by the arm and steadied her.

By the time the morning sun rose at the horizon, coloring the sky reddish and orange, both trekkers were exhausted and ready to give up.

"Are we going to die here?" Lillian asked and turned her desperate eyes to Sawyer.

"No, don't give up. That's the worst thing you can do now," Sawyer replied grimly. If they stayed here, they would certainly die. They had to walk as long as they could.

The golden sun climbed up in the sky and shined on the dunes.

First, Lillian thought she saw a mirage. A shadowed area was ahead of them that looked like trees. She stopped and pointed at it. "Do you see what I see, or am I hallucinating?"

Sawyer shaded his eyes with his hand and looked in the direction where Lillian was pointing. "Yes, there's an oasis. We can't both have the same mirage. Let's go. That place will hopefully be our salvation." He grabbed Lillian by the hand, and they walked with renewed eagerness toward the oasis.

3

THE OASIS

The closer Roy Sawyer and Lillian walked, the more beautiful and alluring the oasis looked. It was like a paradise in the desert. The palm trees swayed in the morning breeze and the vegetation on the ground was thick.

"If there is that much vegetation, there is plenty of fresh water," Sawyer said, and his determined voice made Lillian straighten her shoulders and lift her chin. She could make it there. She knew she would survive with the oasis in their sight.

Sawyer tried to determine how big it was, but he couldn't see around it, so it would take some time for them to walk around or through it when they were ready to leave it behind. They should consider packing water and fruits when leaving the oasis.

The water should be drinkable because plants were growing in this area. It had to be some underground stream. Sawyer wondered if the locals had built wells to get the water.

Meanwhile, when Sawyer had been deep in his thoughts, he had not noticed that Lillian had slowed down. She tilted her head and stared at the oasis.

"What is it?" Sawyer asked her and put her arm over her shoulders.

"It was just something I read in an ancient papyrus scroll back at the German archeologists' camp near the tomb excavation area." Lillian asked, "What date is it?"

"It's the fourteenth of February." Sawyer quickly realized the importance of the date and added, "Happy Valentine's Day!"

Lillian glanced at him and said, "What shape do you think this oasis is?"

"I don't know. I tried to measure it, but it looks big, miles, I would guess," Sawyer commented, surveying the area ahead.

"Would you say that it could be fourteen by fourteen kilometers?" Lillian asked.

Sawyer did a quick calculation in his mind. "Fourteen kilometers is about eight and a half miles. Yes, it could be that size." He glanced at Lillian, his eyebrows raised. "Why? Where did you come up with such specific numbers?"

Lillian sighed and rubbed her forehead with her hand. "The papyrus said the dimensions of a lost oasis of love. It told a story of an oasis that only shows up during the dawn of the fourteenth of February, the day of love and romance. It will disappear from the sight of other travelers and visitors after that narrow window is passed."

"We need to hurry if we want to catch that oasis!" Sawyer said, and they both started running as fast as they could in the treacherous sand.

When they reached the outer limits of the oasis, it looked as if it was growing from the sand. First, there was only sand, and then the green grass and vegetation started. It seemed the oasis was home to a wide variety of plants and flowers. Lillian recognized lilies, pomegranates, belladonnas, and red and white Egyptian stars flowering there and some others that she did not recognize. She wished she had a notebook with her, so she could illustrate some of the plants she saw there and draw pictures of the oasis. It would be a valuable addition to the records of this oasis and would prove that it existed. It was lucky they had arrived here on this particular day and time. They would not have discovered it otherwise.

Lillian's partner, Sawyer, was more interested in finding something to eat and drink. His keen eyes already noticed some edible fruits and vegetables, including pomegranate, date, and coconut palms.

They walked together into the green grass of the oasis and left the dunescape behind.

4

LILLIAN AND SAWYER

"If this is visible on Valentine's Day and only during the morning hours, then we were extremely lucky to find it," Sawyer commented as they walked under the shady trees toward the center of the oasis.

"We needed to find it. Otherwise, we would have died," Lillian said, but her voice was hesitant as if she knew something she was not telling him.

Sawyer noticed the change in her voice and asked, "What is it? Do you know something about this oasis that you're not telling me?" He pulled Lillian in front of him, put his arms around her, and stared at her beautiful eyes. Lillian's hair was sand-covered and sweaty, but she was still very beautiful in his eyes.

Sighing, Lillian put her hand on his chest and stopped him from kissing her. "Stop. I must tell you something. This is not a normal oasis. It's enchanted." Lillian wanted to kiss Sawyer as much as he wanted to, but in this place, it was dangerous and could lead to choices she was not ready to make yet. "Do you know what this oasis is called?"

"The lost oasis of love. You told me that." Sawyer tried to pull Lillian closer, but she resisted.

"Yes, the keyword is *love*. This place is shaped like a heart. It only appears on Valentine's Day and is only visible for a few hours in the morning. The measurements of this island are fourteen by fourteen, like the fourteenth day of this month." Lillian kept her eyes on Sawyer's as she explained it to him. "This is the lost paradise where Adam and Eve supposedly fell in love with each other and also where this world started. It's paradise on earth, but we humans are not supposed to find it or be here. If we stay too long, we will be part of the lost paradise, and we won't be able to return to our world."

"How long is too long?" Sawyer asked, still focusing on Lillian's lips instead of her eyes.

"When the sun sets, we need to be out of here," Lillian replied sternly. "Twelve hours, I guess, is the limit. I don't know for sure, but if this shows at dawn and disappears when the sun sets, then that's all the time we have."

"We need to gather food and water before we leave," Sawyer replied, trying to resist his urge to kiss her.

"And what's more, you can't kiss me here because then we are bound to this paradise," Lillian warned and pulled herself away from him.

"Are you sure you know what you are talking about?" Sawyer asked, frustrated. "This could be another oasis."

Lillian thought about the answer for a moment. "It could be, but I don't think so. We need to be careful if this is the lost paradise on earth. Other things are dangerous to us. We'll have twelve hours to spend here, but when the last sun rays hit the dunes outside this oasis, we must be outside its perimeters. It's important to remember that.

If we stay here, we will disappear with it to wherever it vanishes for the rest of the year. I guess we might come back a year later, but I don't know if we will be the same or if we will age or stay the same age or what happens when this oasis vanishes."

"I don't know if staying here even that long is safe." Sawyer glanced around. Was this oasis safe? Perhaps there was someone like Dina here? Everything looked calm as they stood in the middle of the flowering bushes. He feared now that there were more sinister creatures lurking in the shadows. What if they were not alone here? What if someone or something was watching them? What if they were prohibited from leaving the oasis? They would be stuck there, perhaps forever. He felt icy hands traveling up and down his spine. This place could be paradise, but it was also cursed. He was sure of it.

While Sawyer's senses were on high alert, Lillian felt it too. Something or someone was here with them. They were not alone. She swiveled around but didn't see anyone. She raised her face upwards and saw the sun higher up in the sky. It wasn't late yet. They could still get water and fruits to take with them and leave this place. "Twelve hours," she repeated and turned to walk on the path that led forward. She guessed that if there was a path, others had used it before them. It had to lead somewhere. Sawyer followed her, keeping his senses on alert and his eyes on the sides of the path so that no creature could attack them without him seeing it first.

5

NEHUSHTAN

Despite the balmy morning breeze, Sawyer felt chilled. He was sure something or someone was following them, but he couldn't see anything in the shades of the bushes. He didn't think it was a human. It was something smaller, slithering along the side of the path.

Lillian turned and whispered, "Do you feel that, too? Like someone is watching and following us?"

Sawyer nodded but did not turn his eyes away from the side of the path. He thought he saw the branches moving even when the wind was not blowing. Now, he knew where their follower was. He put his forefinger on his lips and nodded toward the bushes on their left side. Lillian froze in place and didn't move.

With a lightning-fast speed, Sawyer jumped forward and pushed the vegetation and the branches away to see who was following them. What he saw was something he was not prepared for. An enormous snake. Bigger than anything he had ever seen.

He quickly backed away from the bushes back to the path and grabbed Lillian by the arm. "RUN!" he shouted.

When they were still within hearing distance, they heard a lilting voice coming from behind them. "No need to run."

Sawyer turned his head and looked behind his shoulder. The huge snake was now partly on the path and slithered towards them, his mouth open, showing his slit tongue, and his fangs were long, white, and sharp.

Sawyer knew that only venomous snakes had fangs; thus, this gigantic snake was poisonous. Its width was the same as the human's waist, its head was the size of a dog's skull, and Sawyer couldn't even see how long it was as its tail continued behind the bushes. The snake was black with a reddish diamond-shaped pattern running along its back and two yellow diagonal lines on each side of its face running from the eyes to its jaws. His eyes were red around the edges, but the iris was green with slit pupils.

How can a snake talk? Sawyer thought and backed away from the snake in front of Lillian, protecting her with his own body.

"Yes, I can talk," the snake said and glided slowly toward the two humans. "It's been ages since I've seen humans. Perhaps centuries," the snake said thoughtfully, and his tongue moved in and out of his mouth.

"Who are you?" Sawyer asked.

"I'm Chrysopelea paradisi," the snake answered, his head hovering five feet up from the path. "I'm called Nehushtan."

Lillian swallowed and put her hand over her mouth. She recognized the name because of her bible and archeological studies. Moses had a staff which had a metal serpent mounted on his staff that he had made, according to God's command, to cure the Israelites of snake bites while wandering in the desert. According to the bible, Nehushtan was the metal serpent's name. So, if that was truly that snake illustrated in Moses's staff, then this was Eden, the paradise where Adam and Eve once lived, she thought. Could it be true that the lost oasis of love was also the lost Eden on earth?

Sawyer had heard of these snakes during his smuggling journeys to Asia. Usually, they were not seen in Africa, but this oasis was special. Even though its coloring was different from the usual Chrysopelea paradisi snakes, if this snake was one of those snakes, it meant it could glide and fly. These snakes could jump from treetops and guide their bodies in such a way as to float maximum distances of over three hundred feet. Sawyer realized that they couldn't run from it if it decided to attack. So, he stopped and waited patiently for the snake to explain what he wanted from them.

"Welcome to Eden," Nehushtan said, and his eyes were locked on the humans in front of him.

"Thank you," Sawyer said politely. "We don't plan to stay long. We need some water and fruits to bring with us, and then we will leave."

Nehushtan considered the answer for a moment, then said, "Eden is a lovely place to live. You might not want to leave when you see what it has to offer. Besides, it has been ages since I had any human company here."

Sawyer raised his eyebrows. He had not understood that this snake was the snake from the bible like Lillian had, so Lillian nudged him by his elbow and whispered, "Do you know who that is? It's the snake from the bible. It was the one in Eden with Adam and Eve and illustrated in Moses's staff."

"Are you sure?" Sawyer asked and rubbed his chin with his fingers.

"Yes, he said his name. He is the one," Lillian confirmed, keeping her eyes on the snake.

"What should we do?" Sawyer asked his eyes on Nehushtan.

"Let's find the water and some food and leave," Lillian said and backed away carefully.

"Okay, I'm with you," Sawyer said and addressed the snake. "We'll go now to find some water."

"I will catch up with you later," Nehushtan replied, and everything he said sounded ominous as if they were veiled threats.

Lillian kept backing away from the snake, and Sawyer followed. The snake stayed behind and watched them. They both knew that the snake knew this oasis better than they did, so Nehushtan could easily find them if he wanted to.

6

THE WALK

Sawyer kept checking behind them when they hurried along the path that led to the center of the oasis, or so they thought. The vegetation was thick, and the multicolored flowers were abundant on the side of the path.

"I have never seen so many amazingly beautiful and colorful flowers," Lillian said and wished again she had a camera or a notepad to draw them. She decided she would take a couple of samples of the flowers she didn't recognize. Perhaps they were rare, and she could ask around to see if someone knew them. Besides, if this was the lost paradise, the oasis of love, then this place might have plants no one had seen for centuries.

"Yes, there's a lot of them," Sawyer replied half-heartedly. He was more interested in keeping an eye on the snake and the side of the path so they could not be attacked. He had no idea if there would be any other threats here than the huge snake, but he didn't want to risk their lives by being careless.

Nehushtan had not acted dangerously or threateningly when he spoke to them, but a snake was a snake. *I would not trust him,* Sawyer thought. If he was the snake from paradise, then Eve should not have listened to him.

He was Satan, and he deceived Eve; Sawyer recalled the story of Adam and Eve. He wanted Adam and Eve to sin and thus destroy man and cause suffering to God, who created Adam and Eve. Eve ate the fruit of the tree of knowledge of good and evil and, thus, disobeyed God. *If we take fruits from this place, we should not pick from that tree,* Sawyer realized. He slowed his pace and asked Lillian, "Do you remember anything about Adam and Eve?"

"Why do you ask?" Lillian raised her eyebrows. It was strange that Sawyer wanted to talk about the first man and woman now.

"First, because of the snake we met. Second, I recall that Adam and Eve were banished from the garden of Eden because they ate the forbidden fruit from the tree of knowledge of good and bad. I don't want to eat from that tree. I think it would be a horrible idea," Sawyer replied.

Lillian looked thoughtful. "The ancient scrolls did not say what the fruit was. It was only translated later by the Christians to an apple tree because evil is malum and an apple is a malus in Latin. It seemed to fit. However, the earlier pictures showed the fruit of the knowledge to be a fig."

"We stay away from apples and figs then," Sawyer decided. "We can take coconuts, dates, and pomegranates. I see plenty of those here. I have not seen any fig or apple trees," he said.

Lillian said, "It might not be that simple. Hebrew Bible describes the forbidden fruit only as a peri; the term is a general fruit. Perhaps, it's something that does not exist in our world. There have been wild speculations of what that fruit could have been. Some leading researchers assumed it could be a pomegranate, a mango, a fig, or a pear. All are of good size for a bite because Eve took a bite from the apple, so it could not have been a grape. I think it should be a bigger fruit."

"Oh no, we need to cross off pomegranates as well." Sawyer looked disappointed. "Are you sure we can eat date and coconuts?"

"I can't be absolutely sure of anything, but I don't recall any researcher mentioning them."

"We should have asked the snake. Perhaps, Nehushtan would have told them. Even if it had told them a lie, it would have revealed something, Sawyer thought and considered going back and asking the snake.

"Let's go. We don't have many hours left," Lillian said and continued along the path. Sawyer shrugged and followed her. She was right, they did not have much time to spend here. The gravel crunched under their feet. The foliage was thick and lush green, and after a few more steps, Lillian and Sawyer found themselves looking at an opening with a waterfall and a heart-shaped lagoon.

7

THE CAVE

In no time, Roy Sawyer and Lillian Stiller reached the sandy beach surrounding part of the lagoon. Sawyer grabbed the water by the handful and drank it. Then he took off his shirt, shoes, and pants, ran into the water, and dived under. "Ahh! This is awesome!" he said when he came back up on the surface and swam back toward the beach. "The water tastes good, too," he added. Sawyer knew that Lillian was going to ask about that. They were both parched and ready to pass out because of no water.

While Sawyer had rushed to drink the water, Lillian was more cautious. She knew this oasis and the lagoon were not as safe as they had hoped. When Sawyer assured that the water was drinkable, she walked to the waterline, took some of it in her hands, drank it, then took some more and drank slowly this time. She knew she should not drink too much too fast, but she was so thirsty! Then she washed her face. She took off her skirt and boots but left her shirt on and walked into the water too. It felt heavenly after all the sand of the sandstorm.

Sawyer decided to swim to the waterfall. The lagoon was not that deep or large, so it was an easy swim for him. When he got there, he noticed a cave behind the thin veil of water. He disappeared behind the water veil and pulled himself up onto the cave's stony floor. He looked around. Some drawings on the wall interested him. *Lillian should see this,* Sawyer thought and returned to the other side of the waterfall.

Lillian was already looking for him. She had not seen where he had gone.

"I'm here!" Sawyer shouted to her and waved his hand.

Lillian swam to him and said, "Please, don't disappear like that again. It scared me that you had left me alone here."

"Come! I want you to see something," Sawyer led Lillian behind the water veil into the cave. Some light filtered through the waterfall into the cave. There were also some gems and bioluminescent plants on the floor and the cave walls that gave off an eerie greenish light, so it was not completely dark.

Lillian's eyes latched on the wall drawings. She walked there and studied them. For the tenth time, she wished she had her camera or a drawing pad and pen. Now the only thing she could do was to memorize what she saw here.

Her fingers trailed the drawings. "The beginning is here. Adam and Eve in paradise. Then the snake and the fruit of the forbidden tree of good and bad. Then the couple is sent away from Eden." She stopped, turned to Sawyer, and said, "This is Eden, the lost paradise. Someone has told the story here." She moved forward and saw something more disturbing. "The animals that stayed behind started eating each other. Now they were no longer friends but enemies.

And then, I don't understand this next picture," she said, puzzled.

"I can help you," a strange voice said behind them, and both Lillian and Sawyer turned to see who spoke. It was a baboon with fierce-looking canine teeth. He was grey and old, and his eyes looked sad. Slowly, he moved closer to the humans and stared at them wonderingly. "It's been ages since I saw humans."

"Not since Adam and Eve," Lillian replied.

The baboon nodded. "Yes, you're correct." Then he turned to the wall drawings and said, "You asked about the last pictures. It's simple. The animals became enemies. The lions learned that they liked meat instead of veggies and fruits, fresh flesh, and blood. The tigers preferred to hunt and kill too. So, they all made a pact: only one of each animal species can be killed." The baboon moved to the next drawing. "When we had only one of each species, we had to get creative on how to reproduce. So, the solution was that we mix-breed. Now, we have ligers, a crossbreed between a male tiger and a female lion. We have a ganglion crossbreed of a female lion and a male jaguar and a leopon bred by a female lion and a male leopard. A zebroid is, of course, born of a zebra and a horse and coywolf of a coyote and a wolf, and so on. Only those animals who had a lifespan of hundreds of years, like some turtles and parrots, did not want to start mixing with the other species."

The baboon's lecture on what had happened during the past centuries was interesting but also horrifying to Lillian. Then he realized there were two humans, namely Sawyer and herself. "Now there are two humans. What will happen to us?"

The baboon revealed his sharp canines as if smiling and said, "If you don't get out of here soon while you still can, there will be only one of you left. This oasis needs only one human—like it has only one of all the other species."

Lillian swallowed hard, turned to Sawyer, and said, "We should go now." Then she turned to the baboon and said, "Thank you for explaining the drawings. Who did these?"

"I did. I wanted the rest of the world, or whoever comes after I'm gone, to know what happened in this oasis," the baboon replied with a sad voice. "We are killers here. It's not a healthy or friendly place to live. You'll start regretting your life when you've been here for centuries. I gave up living outside a long time ago. This cave is my home now. I did not want to partake in the carnage of the travelers who found this place because every year, someone discovered it, and yet, no one ever knew about this oasis. Now you know why."

"Because they are all dead," Sawyer replied. "Whoever comes here is doomed to die if they stay here."

The baboon nodded. "Correct. You are safe only for the first twelve hours. If you are still here, you'll be as good as dead when the sun sets."

Lillian nudged Sawyer by his arm and said, "We must go now. We've spent here a too long time."

"Goodbye and good luck," the baboon said and withdrew back into the shadows of the cave.

After leaving the cave, Sawyer and Lillian swam back to the beach and got dressed. "We need to find something to eat and then grab water to bring with us," Lillian said.

"How can we carry the water? We don't have any bottles?" Lillian asked.

"I saw something at the bottom of the lagoon," Sawyer said and dived back into the water. He swam around a little bit, went back up to breathe, and then returned to search for what he had seen and saw it again. A pile of skeletons, clothes, and other items. He swam there and picked out a couple of leather decanters. He picked them with him as well as a woven basket, returned to the surface, and headed back to the beach. "These will do," he said and showed his discovery to Lillian.

Sawyer crouched by the waterline, opened the caps of the decanters, filled the bottles with the lagoon's water, and closed the caps tightly. The bottles were still good because they were leather and could not be broken. He stood up and showed them to Lillian. "See, these old bottles hold water, and we can carry them with the string over our shoulders."

Lillian nodded, smiling. "That water won't last very long, but I hope if we ration it, it will be enough." She started thinking that they could survive this place after all. Gazing upward, Lillian saw that the sun was already moved past the high noon. *It must be afternoon*, she thought. *Not many hours left, and we still need to find food and a way out.* Lillian tied her hair into a ponytail so it would not be in her way.

"What fruits do you think we should take with us?" Sawyer asked. He had the basket in his hands and the filled bottles hanging over his shoulders.

"I would pick up dates and coconuts," Lillian said, adding, "I also saw some pineapples."

"Okay, fine with me," Sawyer said and brushed a wet curl away from his forehead. "As long as we don't pick up the fruit of the tree of knowledge of good and bad."

"That's the problem," Lillian said, frowning. "We don't know for sure what it is. I studied the drawings in the cave, and to me, it looked like a round fruit. It could be an apple, pomegranate, or fruit we don't have in our world. So, I think we should avoid any round fruit if we see one," Lillian replied.

"Ah, you did pay attention in the cave. I tried to figure out the fruit in the drawings too, but I think the baboon made it unclear so that no one would know for sure what the fruit was," Sawyer said. Then he pointed ahead. "I would avoid the path we came in because of the snake. I don't know what we'll see if we go that route, but I would rather go there than talk to the snake again."

"Fine with me," Lillian replied, shivering. She had not liked the snake either. It looked like it was hiding something or deliberately telling them certain things so they would not suspect whatever it told them.

8

THE WAY OUT OR NOT?

As Sawyer and Lillian walked away from the lagoon, Sawyer kept his eyes on the ground. He had not told Lillian that he had seen multiple paw prints on the ground. Now, he kept looking forward and stopped when he saw fewer pawprints heading in their direction. He crouched down and pressed his fist on the ground, measuring the pawprint's size. It was enormous, almost twice the size of his fist. The cat who had made that print was bigger than any lions he had hunted in Africa before the war.

Lillian watched Sawyer as he studied the pawprints. "What is wrong?" She looked worried.

Sawyer turned his head to her, and his eyes were serious. "I don't think we should go that way. If we meet that cat, he could easily kill us. We don't have any weapons. A cat that size is bigger than I have ever seen." He looked around, then said, "Let's cut through the vegetation. Perhaps, that's better than following the path." He thought that if that was one of the mix-breed cats, a liger or a ganglion, he would not want to see it. A mix-breed could be dangerous, even evil.

Sawyer walked first, pushing away the branches and the ground vegetation and Lillian followed him. After they had walked for a good ten minutes, Sawyer stopped. He had seen something in the corner of his eye. A movement. He held his hand at his side, telling Lillian to stop and stay behind him. His eyes canvassed the vegetation and the palms ahead and next to them. And there it was again! A colorful blur of motion flew from one tree to another. He relaxed. A red-green parrot!

As they stood still, the parrot flew closer, sat on the stone ahead of them, and opened its beak. "Good afternoon. Can I be of any assistance?"

Sawyer relaxed his protective position, and Lillian smiled. "Good afternoon. I don't know if you can help us," she replied.

"What do you need?" the parrot asked, tilting his head from side to side.

"We need to get some fruits and coconuts to take with us, and after that, we will leave this oasis," Lillian replied.

The parrot's friendly demeanor changed in a second. It flew up and shrieked, "The humans are here! Come and get them before they leave."

"Let's run!" Sawyer said and led Lillian on a wild run through the vegetation back to the lagoon.

When they got there, he stopped and glanced around. "Everything looks calm. What should we do next?"

"Let's not go that way again," Lillian replied, panting. "I think we should go and talk to the baboon in the cave and ask how to find a way out of here."

"Good idea. Do you want to wait here or come with me?" Sawyer asked, lowering the basket and the bottles to the ground next to a tall palm tree and taking off his boots.

"I'll come with you. I don't want to be alone here, not even for a minute," Lillian replied sternly and took off her boots. She glanced at the water bottles and said, "We should keep those with us. What if we can't return to this side of the lagoon, or a liger is waiting for us next to our bottles and clothes?"

Sawyer replied, "I'll cut some branches to put over our boots and the basket. We'll keep our clothes on." He leaned over, cut off some branches from the nearby plants with enormous elephant-ear leaves, and covered their belongings under them. "I hope they are safe now," he added, taking a few steps backward to assess their cache under the leaves. It looked like a pile of large leaves, nothing else.

"It looks good from a distance. I don't think the animals will take them if they are not visible," Lillian said, hoping it was true. The animals and birds in the oasis were nothing like normal ones.

Sawyer and Lillian walked into the water, swam to the waterfall, and entered the cave again.

9

THE BABOON AND THE WAY OUT

The grey baboon sat near the opening as if he had been waiting for them to return.

As Sawyer and Lillian emerged through the waterfall's veil, he glanced up. He was drawing another picture on the wall. This time it depicted two humans and animals surrounding them.

Gasping, Lillian noticed the drawing and nudged Sawyer, who looked at it. He saw a way out. The animals were not in a full circle. There was a path through the mountain, a tunnel of caves leading to the other side of the oasis. That would mean they would have to leave their boots and basket behind. Or could they go and fetch them? Sawyer turned and looked through the waterfall and saw shadows appearing around the lagoon, some bigger and others smaller. They all gathered around the lagoon as if waiting for them to come back. The parrot had done its surveillance job and squealed at every predator on this island.

Lillian asked the baboon, "Are you going to stop us if we use the cave system to get out?"

"No, I'm not. I wondered if you would come back. The oasis is full of dangers. Here you'll have just me." The baboon opened his mouth wide, showing his sharp yellow canine teeth. He stood up slowly and then banged his chest and let out a high-pitched scream.

Gasping in fear, Lillian stepped backward on the cave's floor, leaning on the wall, but Sawyer took a step forward. "Are you going to fight me?"

The baboon looked at him, puzzled. "No, I'm shouting to let the others know that you are mine and I'm taking care of you. That's the only way for you to pass the cave system so others don't come here and follow you."

Relaxing, Sawyer asked, "Can you show us the way out?"

The baboon stared outside through the waterfall for a while, then said, "Go through back there. You'll find a passage through the caves. Follow it until you reach the edge of the oasis, then run! You're almost out of time."

Sawyer grabbed Lillian by the hand, and they walked fast to the end of the cave and then followed a narrow path that seemed to twist and turn inside the mountain. It took them several hours to see a light ahead in the tunnel.

"We are almost out!" Sawyer said encouragingly. He knew that Lillian must be exhausted by now. They had not had time to find any fruits or coconuts to eat. She had not had anything to eat for two days, and neither had he. He swore that before they left this oasis, he would find some fruits to take with them. They needed them to survive in the desert.

When they got closer to the cave opening on the other side of the mountain, Sawyer saw something sparkling on the ground. The sand had piled around the mouth of the cave, but the recent storm must have revealed the coins under the sand. He crouched down and brushed the sand away. Several old coins were there. He moved more sand away and also found a jewel-decorated dagger, which he put in his belt loop.

The dagger could come in handy if I have to fight our way out, Sawyer thought grimly. Then he grabbed the coins in his hand. He stood up, opened his palm, and showed the coins to Lillian.

Fascinated like always with a new archeological discovery, Lillian picked one up and said, "This looks like a denarius, an old Roman Empire coin." She turned the coin in her hand and read the name aloud. "Brutus EID Mar." She handed it back to Sawyer and said, "These coins might be worth a fortune. Keep them safe in your pocket. If we ever get out of here, I want to look at them more closely."

Lillian didn't tell Sawyer that she had never seen a gold denarius with Brutus's name on it. *It must be worth a lot of money to collectors*, Lillian thought.

10

NEHUSHTAN

Keeping the dagger in his right hand, Sawyer went to look outside.

The mountain sloped to the small strip of oasis, then behind that, Sawyer could see the desert and the endless dunescape. *That's where we are heading*, he thought. *Not too far to go.*

They were now on the other side of the mountain with their water bottles, but they had no boots. They would need food too. Sawyer thought about wrapping pieces of fabric around their feet when they got to the desert, so their feet would not burn. Perhaps, he could also take some of those elephant-ear leaves and wrap them around their feet first and then the fabric.

"It looks safe," Sawyer said and held out his left hand to Lillian, who grabbed it. Sawyer's eyes surveyed the palms and the bushes ahead of them. "Walk carefully. I don't want any cuts on your feet bleeding," he warned Lillian. Any blood drops could alert the wild animals in the oasis, which would not be good.

Per his advice, Lillian walked slowly and cautiously and let Sawyer keep an eye on the hostile environment.

When they stood next to the first palm trees, they heard a voice above, "My new humans! How nice of you to make an excursion around the oasis. How do you like it so far?"

Lillian jumped backward and turned her head upwards to the top of the palm tree where the sound had come from. And there he was: Nehushtan! She shivered. They had not fooled the snake. He was clever. The snake had guessed they would try to avoid the big cats and go through the caves.

Lillian's heart pounded as if she was running a marathon. She tried to calm herself down and took a few deep breaths.

Sawyer stared at the gigantic snake whose black body wound around the top of the tree, and he could see its reddish diamond-shaped pattern on its back as it lowered down and hung almost to their head level. Sawyer stared at the slit pupils and wondered if it was a real snake or an evil spirit.

Nehushtan opened his mouth wide, showing his fangs and forked tongue as he spoke. "I came here to wait for you. I was sure you didn't want to leave without saying goodbye." His body swayed as he gazed at them. His mouth was so big that he could easily swallow a human.

"We didn't expect to see you again," Lillian said politely, pulling Sawyer away from the palm tree where the snake hung its head.

"It almost looked like you were trying to escape this oasis," Nehushtan said, lowering his body smoothly along the palm trunk.

"We are looking for edible fruits and vegetables," Sawyer offered when he noticed Lillian slowly backing away.

"Food. You are hungry," Nehushtan said with a lilting voice as he came down another two feet. "Let me show you some edible fruits."

Nehushtan slithered down the trunk, keeping his head raised. His heavy body moved smoothly across the path where Lillian and Sawyer stood. Both kept their eyes on the snake.

It's a trickster, Lillian thought. *It's not a snake but something eviler.*

Nehushtan curled around one tree, which was not a palm tree, but looked like a pomegranate tree, and said, "These are delicious fruits. If I were you, I'd pick these and eat before they are too ripe and fall onto the ground." His blunt head swayed back and forth as if it tried to manipulate or hypnotize them.

Lillian glanced at the tree and said, "Thank you. It was kind of you to show this tree to us. We won't bother you anymore. I'm sure you are very busy."

It looked like the snake squinted his eyes. He knew Lillian was trying to get rid of him. He curled around the trunk and stayed there watching them. "I can wait."

Sawyer kept his eyes on the surroundings. He didn't want to stay here longer than they had to.

This snake is trying to keep us here past sunset, Sawyer realized. He grabbed Lillian by her arm and pulled her away along the path, and said, "We need to go." He didn't want to play cat and mouse with Nehushtan when they were almost out of time. If they stayed any longer, they would be stuck here for another year or perhaps forever.

Sawyer took Lillian's hand, and they ran away. When Nehushtan saw this, he attacked.

His body flew in the air and hit the tree trunk ahead of them. The snake had jumped or flown like Sawyer knew it could do. Now Nehushtan stared at them ahead of the path they had chosen. His thick body moved steadily towards them, and his eyes were latched on the two humans. And then it attacked!

His blunt head and massive body flew towards them, his mouth open and his fangs dripping venom. Sawyer and

Lillian dived to the side of the path and barely avoided the direct hit. Nehushtan turned his blunt head and saw where they escaped. "There you are, my little pets," he cooed, getting ready for the second strike.

Sawyer saw his chance. He had the dagger hidden behind his back and whispered to Lillian, "Run left when I say now."

He kept his eyes on Nehushtan, and when he saw the snake was ready, he yelled, "Now!" when the snake attacked, he jumped to the left, cutting the snake's side with the dagger and injuring one of his eyes. Lillian ran as she was told, stopping to see what had happened behind her.

The blood poured from Nehushtan's injured side, and his eye was blind and bloody.

Nehushtan screamed in pain and trashed his body. "You cut me! You hurt me! I will kill you!" The bushes and trees swayed when the snake's heavy body hit them, and Nehushtan broke several branches with his trashing.

Sawyer snuck to the side where Nehushtan's good eye was and jumped up to poke his other eye. His moves were sure and swift. He had used daggers before.

The snake screamed! "You blinded me! I will kill you."

Sawyer ran away, grabbed Lillian's hand, and kept going across the rest of the oasis where he had seen the desert. They ran fast as they could and did not care if they cut themselves or their feet. It was safer to get out of this place than let any other animal strike and eat them.

11

THE LAST DAY IN THE OASIS

Nehushtan's cries and trashing alerted the other animals, and soon Sawyer and Lillian heard big cats roaring and heavy steps running after them. Hooves and claws, Sawyer thought. The cats were not the only weird creatures in this oasis.

A crack appeared in the ground in front of them, growing rapidly.

Sawyer saw it first and shouted, "We need to jump over it."

The path winded past the tall vegetation with huge leaves and beautiful flowers. The tall palm trees swayed above them.

Sawyer headed in the direction he had seen from the mountain, where the dunes were.

They rushed ahead, Sawyer pulling Lillian by the hand after him and not letting her fall behind. With the last of their strength, they leaped across the widening crevice. Sawyer got to the other side, but Lillian failed. She hung over the edge, screaming in terror when she saw the depths of the gap. It was fire and burning lava.

"Help! Don't let me fall," she pleaded, turning her eyes to Sawyer and digging her fingers into the stones on the edge of the crevice. Sawyer had her hand still in his and pulled her up to the other side slowly and steadily. She rolled over the edge and panted. "Thank you. You saved my life. Lillian turned her scared eyes to him, but his eyes were fixed across the widening gap.

All the animals had gathered there: big cats, weird creatures with hooves and horns, and other snakes. Even Nehushtan slithered back there with his bleeding eyes.

The animals watched the crack widen, but none tried to jump after them. Sawyer was sure it would happen soon. "Let's go. We don't have any time to waste." He pulled Lillian up, and they continued running.

Sawyer heard a cry behind as one of the big cats tried to leap over the gap in the ground, and it fell to red hot lava. Sawyer looked back and saw it happen and how the other animals paced along the edge of the gap. They were afraid to jump after the bravest of them fell.

Sawyer glanced up at the top of the palm trees, worried. If the oasis had predatory birds, then their fate was sealed. He didn't see any and hoped they would not show up until they were clear.

They had only a few hundred feet left, then they would reach the dunes and safety.

The red sun was setting in the far distance behind the dunes, the horizon colored orange and yellow.

"Come on!" Sawyer shouted to Lillian, dragging her with him. "We are running out of time. The sun is setting!"

They ran as fast as they could, and when the last rays hit the dunes, their feet touched the dunes.

They felt the ground shake under their feet, stumbled forward, and fell onto the burning-hot sand. They glanced back, and the oasis vanished in front of their eyes. It sunk into the ground and disappeared. In a few moments, there was nothing left but dunes as far as they could see. No oasis. No monster snakes or big cats.

Lillian rolled to her back and sighed. "Are we safe now?"

Sawyer rolled next to her and said, "Are we ever?"

They both started laughing.

Lillian said, "We have the water from the oasis. Is it still in the bottles?"

Sawyer pulled out one of the bottles from around his neck and opened it. He poured some water into his mouth and said, "Yes, we have water." He gave it to Lillian, who drank it too.

"We don't have anything to eat," Lillian said. "I don't even remember when I ate last time."

"We couldn't have taken anything from the oasis. We didn't know what, if anything, was safe." Sawyer sat up.

"Let me wrap a piece of my shirt around your feet. They're bleeding."

Lillian glanced at her feet. "I didn't even notice that." Sawyer took off his long sleeve shirt, ripped the sleeves, and wrapped them around her feet. Then he cut his pant legs off with his dagger and tied them around his feet.

"Okay, now we are ready to go," he said and stood up and extended his hand to Lillian, and when she grabbed it, he pulled Lillian up and against his chest. He held her tight and looked deeply into her eyes. "I love you, Lillian. I want you to know that. You said I couldn't kiss you back in the oasis, but we are not there now."

He lowered his lips to hers and held her tighter. Lillian shivered. This was what she wanted; to be in his arms. Their burning kiss continued for a long time as if they didn't even care for the rest of the world and the imminent danger, they were still in.

Sighing, Lillian pulled away and looked at Sawyer's eyes. "Are you sure you did not kiss me because of the water of the lost oasis?"

Sawyer laughed. "No, definitely not. I wanted to kiss you before we ended up in that wretched place."

Lillian smiled. "You know, I remember reading that the water of the lost oasis can give you a healthier and longer life."

Sawyer stared at her eyes, and his fingers traced her face when he said, "And love."

"And love," Lillian repeated, smiling. She took Sawyer's hand, and they turned to face the horizon.

They walked ahead under the starry sky, heading toward the north star, hoping to see something familiar or find a caravan or any other travelers.

Lillian was exhausted when the morning sun rose and collapsed on the sand. Sawyer sat next to her. She had been a real trooper and kept walking all night, even though he knew Lillian must be exhausted. He was deeply worried. They would die here if they did not find any help. They didn't have any hats, and the sun would be scorching hot soon. *A full day in the hot sand will be our end*, he thought grimly.

And right then, when his thoughts were the worst, he heard a familiar voice shouting and a car horn honking. "Hello there. Do you want a ride?"

"Jack!" Lillian whispered. She looked up and saw Jack's Jeep riding towards them.

Sawyer got up and waved at him.

When Jack stopped next to them, he noticed Lillian's condition. "Let's get you in the car," he said, half-carrying her to the vehicle and placing her in the back seat. He gave her a scarf to protect her from the heat.

Sawyer followed the siblings and sat next to Jack in front. Jack came to the driver's side and asked, "I've been looking for you for two days. Where were you?"

He started the car and glimpsed at Sawyer, who said, "We found a lost oasis. We were lost there for a day after the sandstorm."

"A lost oasis?" Jack said, shaking his head. "I want to hear that story. I was so worried. I thought you were dead." He drove back, heading to Cairo. He had his compass with him, so it was easy for him to find his way.

"Where did you go when the sandstorm hit? We couldn't find you or the Jeep anywhere," Sawyer asked, glancing back at Lillian, who lay in the back seat. Her eyes were open, and she was listening to them.

Jack chuckled. "I had my own adventure. I fell into a stone tunnel next to the tomb. I stayed there while the storm raged, and when it stopped, I walked out. I found the Jeep next to the tomb, but I couldn't see you anywhere."

Sawyer shook his head. "We didn't see you or the Jeep. It was as if we were meant to find the lost oasis."

"Yes, it sounds like it. This desert keeps tricking us. First, Dina, then the venomous dunes, and now you had your adventure in the lost oasis." Jack pulled something out of his shirt pocket and handed it back to Lillian. "I found these for you. These old papyruses were in the tunnel where I fell. I could only translate something about the last war, and the other talks about the only path."

Lillian sat up in the back seat and took the papyruses Jack handed her. "How interesting. Perhaps these are our next adventures."

Sawyer glimpsed at Lillian. "Are you already ready for another adventure?" He asked with a disbelieving voice. "We just got out of that hellhole, and now you want to find another threat to our lives!"

Lillian gave him a wide smile. "Why not? We are alive."

Jack belly-laughed in front. "Let's get you to a hospital to be checked out before any new adventures. You look like you need a good meal and rest."

"You are right, my friend. And after the hospital, bath, rest, and food, I'm ready for the next adventure," Sawyer said patting Jack on the shoulder.

About the Author

Meet Arla Jones, a multi-genre author hailing from the picturesque landscapes of Finland, now making waves in the literary world from the tranquil shores of Michigan. With a penchant for exploring diverse genres, the author captivates readers with tales that traverse the realms of mystery, romance, thriller, sci-fi, and fantasy, weaving intricate narratives that transport audiences to worlds both familiar and fantastical. When not penning captivating stories, the author enjoys gardening and painting.

Also By The Author

Some of these are published as serial fiction and some
are available in different formats.

The Starbound Orphans Series: (YA/Sci-Fi)

Starbound Orphans

Starbound Journey

Starbound Hearts

The Galactic Emperor (coming soon)

The Ackley Family Saga:

Lord Ackley's Choice

A Rose So Red

Court of Kisses

A Romance Short story:

Snowbound Strangers

Jaxon Axis -series (Dystopian, Sci-Fi):

Jaxon Axis and the First Crime

Jaxon Axis and the Ice Age

The Lost Tomb -series:

The Lost Tomb

Venemous Dunes

The Lost Oasis of Love

Mummy Returns

The Otis Thorne Thriller series:

Fathers and Sons

Black Dust

The Facility

Death Walks in Washington D.C.

The Ashburn -series

On Death's Door

Finders Keepers

The Kingdom Series (fantasy, romantasy, YA)

Wings of Sea

Wings of War

Wings of Shadows

Westerns

The Lady and The Stubborn Rancher

The Lady and The Robber Baron

Bury My Dreams

The Cupid and the Elf -series:

Love Trap

Naughty Elf

Ghost Stories

The Cursed Banshee

Don't Go There

Sci-Fi

The Host

Titanic Paranormal Novel

Chasing Death

Children's books:

The Attack of the Iguana

Evil Elves

The Underground Cat Academy

Bobbie Robins Contemporary thrillers:

Samantha Raven Trilogy:

I'll Be Your Shadow

I'll Never Let You Go

I'll Be Back

The Minotaur series:

Minotaur's Muse

Minotaur's Curse

Ariadne's Revenge

Ayla Jones (Dark Romance)

Donder

No Way But Down

Dragon Unleashed

Bloodlines of Revolution

Anthologies:

The Tales of Howloween

Find a full list of serial fiction, novels, and my shop: arlaj

ones.com

And also https://beacons.ai/arlajonesbooks

Tiktok: @jonesesbooks and @authorarlajones

Facebook: www.facebook.com/authorarlajones

Instagram: https://www.instagram.com/arlajonesbooks